THIS
ZOO
IS NOT
FOR
YOU

For Corra and Cairn –
this zoo is for you

First published 2017 by Nosy Crow Ltd
The Crow's Nest, Baden Place, Crosby Row
London SE1 1YW
www.nosycrow.com

This edition published 2017
ISBN 978 0 85763 895 3

A CIP catalogue record for this book
is available from the British Library.
Printed in Turkey
Papers used by Nosy Crow are made from
wood grown in sustainable forests.

10 9 8 7 6 5 4 3 2 1

ROSS COLLINS

THIS ZOO IS NOT FOR YOU

Hello, come in.

How do you do?

Have you come

for the interview?

A platypus!

That's strange and new!

You're meeting Panda first –

go through.

I'm special, rare
and **famous** too.

To get me here
was **quite** a coup.
But you don't even
eat **bamboo!**

I think, this zoo
is **not** for you.

We're elegant and graceful too.
We really do **enhance** the view.

But you look like
a **worn-out shoe.**

And so this zoo
is **not** for you.

We're very good at throwing poo.
Young Jeffrey here can play kazoo.

Is there a trick that you can do?
If not, this zoo
is not for you.

We are a multicoloured crew.
I'm **green**, then **red**,
then **pink**, or **blue**.

You're brownish-grey
– but just **one** hue.

It's clear this zoo
is **not** for you.

I'm powerful
and **huge**, it's true.

You are short
and quite weird too.

You've simply **failed**
this interview.

You see, this zoo
is **not** for you.

How did you find the interview?
I think I was **unkind.** Were you?

Perhaps he **could** have
joined our zoo.

But now he's gone.
What **shall** we do?

We **must** apologise to you –
you didn't **want** to
join our zoo.
We got it **wrong** –
that much is true.

We found your
invitation too!

We'd **love** to be
good friends . . .

. . . would you?

Relax,

guys . . .

This **platybus** is for **all** of us!